Who Woke the Animals?

'FOR ALL THE STAFF AT ST PETER IN CHAINS
RC INFANT SCHOOL' D.C

Who Woke the Animals?

Written by David Conway
Illustrated by Charles Fuge
First published as *Bedtime Hullabaloo* in 2010.
This edition published in 2015 by
Hodder Children's Books

MIX
Paper from
responsible sources
FSC
www.fsc.org
FSC® C104740

'What a hullabaloo!' said the leopard
and decided to follow the noise.

Along the way the leopard passed by a dozy giraffe singing a lullaby when all of a sudden...

HHHRRR-ZZZ!

SNORT, SNORT!

'What a hullabaloo!' said the giraffe
and decided to follow the noise.

The leopard and
the giraffe then met a
baboon who was reading
a bedtime story to the moon
when all of a sudden...

HHHRRR-ZZZ!

SNORT, SNORT!
GRUNT, GRUNT!

'What a hullabaloo!' said the baboon and decided to follow the noise.

The three animals followed the noise
to check out all the fuss and discover
the source of this bedtime din, this
clamour, this hubbub, this rumpus.

Under the still starlit night they walked.
The noise began to swell.

More and more animals joined in the search
to seek out the nuisance as well. There was
a hat-wearing hyena half asleep, a music-making
meerkat counting sheep...

...a zany zebra who was having a dream about sailing upon a sea of ice cream,

a sleepwalking lion with bedraggled hair,
an outraged ostrich clutching a teddy bear,
and a polka-dot-pyjama-wearing water buffalo.

So on they all walked into the night, all sleepy and tired and very uptight. Through the long giggling grass, past the tickling tree,

and when at last they came to a stop what on earth did they see?

Not a raucous
rhinoceros...

or a cacophonous
hippopotamus...

But a tiny shrew, wearing a pink tutu, snoring her head off very loudly.

HHHRRR-ZZZ!

SNORT, SNORT! GRUNT, GRUNT!

Something had to be done. Leopard growled as loud as he could. Giraffe bleated even louder.

Baboon screeched with all his might until...

...the terrible racket woke the shrew from her thunderous slumber.

And all was quiet on the Silly Savannah,
so quiet you couldn't hear a peep...

...until the silence was suddenly shattered by some animals fast asleep in a heap.

R-ZZZ!

SNORT, SNORT!

GRUNT, GRUNT!

SNUFFLE, SNUFFLE!